First Printing, 2019
PRINT ISBN : 978-1949603033
EBOOK ISBN: 978-1-949603-32-3
For questions and ordering information visit:
www.ascanbekids.com
email:info@ascanbekids.com

WITH YOUR PURCHASE TODAY
VISIT THE WEBSITE FOR YOUR
FREE COLORING EBOOK

COLLECT ALL 3 BOOKS

WWW.ASCANBEKIDS.COM

AS SPECIAL AS CAN BE

Dedicated
to the
Special child reading
now

It was a beautiful summer afternoon,
the skies as lovely as could be.
Bigblue Penguin watched closely as
Bittieblue Penguin slowly attempted
some baby steps.

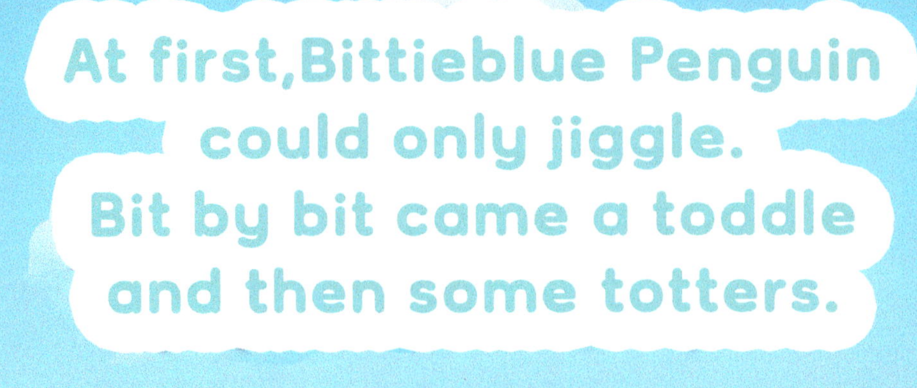
At first,Bittieblue Penguin
could only jiggle.
Bit by bit came a toddle
and then some totters.

Before long, Bittieblue Penguin
was waddling away!

Bigblue Penguin
was heartily
amazed.

"Dazzling, simply dazzling, my little darling,
as dazzling as could be,"
said Bigblue Penguin!"

Bigblue Penguin suggested, "How about we take a few steps through the woods." Bittieblue Penguin was so thrilled and immediately said, "Absolutely."

A few steps into the woods, they caught
a glimpse of a merry monkey.
Like a sling, they watched him swing,
from tree to tree.

Bittieblue Penguin fixed her gaze on him and said to Bigblue Penguin, "If I could swing like that monkey, would that make me more admirable?"

Bigblue Penguin graciously said,
"No, my little darling, you are as admirable
as can be just by being you!"

Along came a lonely camel, carefully dodging the bumps.

He had two huge humps. Bittieblue Penguin thought, and asked, "If I had humps like that, would that make me more valuable?"
Bigblue Penguin smiled and said, "No, my little darling, you are as valuable as can be just by being you!"

At a nearby creek, they dipped their beaks, sipped some water,

and rested their tired feet.

Bittieblue Penguin,
no doubt, had had a treat.

After a while,
they spotted a chameleon,
a far cry from a lion.

Bittieblue Penguin paused and observed; she noticed the chameleon's skin kept changing colors as it moved. She turned and said to Bigblue Penguin, "If I could change colors like that chameleon, would that make me more likable?" Bigblue Penguin gently uttered, "No, my little darling, you are as likable as can be just by being you!"

The sun was beginning
to set amidst a cool evening breeze.
It had been an eventful day.
As they began to head home,
Bittieblue Penguin fixed her gaze
on an eagle.

It was miles and miles away,
high in the sky. Hmmm,
she thought and
asked, "If I could fly
as high as that eagle,
I suppose it would
make me more
honorable."

Bigblue Penguin bent over and looked intently into Bittieblue Penguin's eyes, more deliberately than ever before,

and said, "You are as honorable as can be, just by being you!"

Now, they were about to make
the very last turn through
the clump of shrubs, to their little nest.

Suddenly, a colorful peacock crossed their path, obviously of age, proudly flaunting his plumage. Bittieblue Penguin had never seen such beautiful feathers.

Before Bittieblue Penguin could give voice to any words, Bigblue Penguin tenderly comforted Bittieblue Penguin with these words, "Dear child, you are as precious as can be, just by being you!"

Finally, they were home,
in their very own welcoming, warm nest.

As Bigblue Penguin and Bittieblue Penguin were about to hit the hay, Bittieblue Penguin mumbled one last question, "What makes me special?"

Bittieblue Penguin held on tight, and they nestled as Bigblue Penguin said these profound words, "You are as special as can be - just the way God made you!"

www.ingramcontent.com/pod-product-compliance
Lightning Source LLC
Chambersburg PA
CBHW042109160726
48295CB00017B/1036